P E B B L E

A Story About Belonging

Susan Milord

HarperCollinsPublishers

There once was a pebble on a rocky shore.
It was small and round and nearly smooth.

Each morning
the seabirds sang to the pebble,
and each afternoon
the ocean breezes
gently teased it.

The pebble was warmed by the sun
and bathed by the rain.

On clear nights, it was dazzled by the stars.

Sometimes a storm pounded the shore,
and the sea threw itself over the pebble.

That was exciting, even a little frightening.

Then the winds would die down,
and the sea would retreat,
and the pebble would return
to its small and round
and nearly smooth life.

But the pebble longed for more.

"If I were a boulder," the pebble said,
"I might be part of a stone wall.

Or the foundation of a great building."

"You will never be part of a stone wall
or building," the other rocks pointed out.
"You are too small for that."

"If I were a grain of sand," the pebble said,
"I could be shaped into a sand castle.

Or melted into a piece of glass for a fine window."

"Not in a million years," the other rocks said
with a laugh. "You are too big for that."

"If I had flecks of mica," the pebble said,
"or a blaze of shining white, maybe then
I would be something special."

"Stop dreaming,"
the other rocks advised.
"You are what you are."

The pebble tried hard to accept what the others said.
Still, it felt a longing it could not put a name to.
"There must be more to life than this," the pebble thought.
"But I don't know what."

The pebble gave up trying to understand.
Life was good, after all.
The sky was often a brilliant blue,
and the air tasted of salt.

Scuttling crabs tickled the pebble,
and there was nothing so beautiful
as the full moon dancing
on the water.

But the empty feeling would not go away.

One day, a boy walked along
the shore with his mother and father.
The boy let the seawater swirl around his ankles.
He watched the gulls swoop overhead,
and he laughed as the shell
he was reaching for started to move.

Warmed by the sun and by everything around him,
the boy was filled with a sense of wonder.

When it was time to leave,
the boy asked his parents to wait.
"I won't be long," he told them.
"I just need to find something."

The boy wandered down the beach.
He noticed a smooth shard of beach glass.
"This will remind me of the color
of the sea," the boy said to himself.
But it wasn't quite what he was searching for,
and he put it down.

A little farther along, he spotted a white feather.
"This will remind me of the noisy gulls,"
the boy thought.

But the feather wasn't what he had in mind either.

The boy picked up a shell.
"This will remind me of the
creatures on the shore," he said.

He turned the shell
over and over in his hands,
pondering . . . considering. . . .

And then he saw it.
It was small and round
and nearly smooth.

It fit perfectly in his palm, and the boy knew at once.
"This will be my pocket friend," he said.
"It will remind me always of this wonderful day."

He called out to his mother and father.
"I found what I was looking for!"

The pebble felt the warmth
of the boy's hand all around it.
It glowed with delight as
the boy ran his fingers over
the pebble's smallness and
roundness and nearly smoothness.

The pebble, too, knew at once.

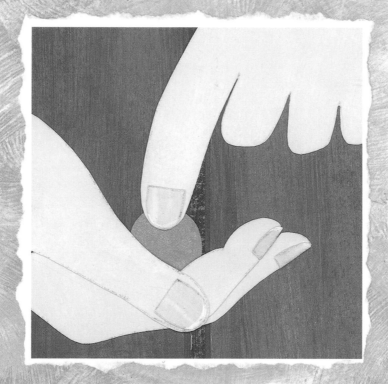

"And I have found what I was looking for."

For my brother, Christian

Pebble: A Story About Belonging
Copyright © 2007 by Susan Milord
Manufactured in China.

Library of Congress Cataloging-in-Publication Data
Milord, Susan.
     Pebble: a story about belonging / Susan Milord.— 1st ed.
         p.   cm.
     Summary: A smooth, round pebble on a rocky shore enjoys life but wishes for something more,
and finds it in the palm of a young child's hand.
     ISBN-10: 0-06-085807-9 (trade bdg.) — ISBN-13: 978-0-06-085807-0 (trade bdg.)
     ISBN-10: 0-06-085808-7 (lib. bdg.) — ISBN-13: 978-0-06-085808-7 (lib. bdg.)
     [1. Pebbles—Fiction. 2. Beaches—Fiction. 3. Self-realization—Fiction.] I. Title.
PZ7.M6445 Peb 2007   2006001125
[E]—dc22   CIP
                                                                             AC

Typography by Carla Weise
1 2 3 4 5 6 7 8 9 10
❖
First Edition